To

Benjamin,

Merry Christmas!

Love from

. . . .

Benjamin sees a present
wrapped up neatly with a bow.
The label says his name,
and the wrapping seems to glow.

"This gift is for me!" cries Benjamin,
with the biggest grin.
He opens it to look inside,
and suddenly falls in!

Benjamin's in the frosty woods.
He can't believe his eyes.
To find a world inside a box
is such a big surprise!

ELF WORKSHOP

NORTH POLE EXPRESS

SANTA'S HOUSE

He stares up at a signpost
to see which way to go.
"Santa's house?" he says in awe,
then runs through sparkly snow.

Benjamin spots a village
and a family up ahead.
When he gets close he gasps because
they're made of gingerbread!

The dad smiles at Benjamin.
"You want Santa's house, I guess?
You'll get there so much quicker
on the ol' North Pole Express."

Benjamin's at the station
when he spots a little elf.
The elf tells him, "I'm off to see
Santa Claus, himself."

Benjamin is excited.
"I'm off to see him too!
But I'm not sure which way to go.
Can I come along with you?"

They hear a distant chugging sound,
then see the train appear.
The elf says, "Look, Benjamin!
The North Pole Express is here!"

ALL ABOARD, BENJAMIN

WELCOME BENJAMIN

NORTH POLE EXPRESS

The elf takes Benjamin to a house.
Mrs. Claus greets him with glee.
"I'm so glad you are here at last.
Come in and sit with me!"

Benjamin sips hot chocolate,
warm cookies fill his plate.
The elf says, "Eat up, Benjamin.
We really can't be late."

Benjamin is led through
a busy workshop full of elves,
where a million shiny toys
sit high on countless shelves.

"Will I see Santa?" Benjamin hopes.
"That would be so neat."
The elf says, "Yes! That's why you're here.
He really wants to meet!"

"Ho ho **hello**, Benjamin!
You've been so good this year.
That's why I left a magic gift—
so I could bring you here!"

to Benjamin

"Yes, you wished to meet me.
I made that wish come true.
And now, I have a special toy.
One I made...just for you."

to Benjamin

Benjamin peeks inside the box,
then quickly lifts his head.
He no longer sees Santa—
but is back at home instead!

His trip has been amazing,
a night he won't forget.
And in the box is Santa's gift:
a North Pole Express train set!

Benjamin, hop onboard the
NORTH POLE EXPRESS!

Draw yourself and your friends
on the train to see Santa.

Written by J.D. Green
Designed by Jane Gollner

Copyright © Hometown World Ltd. 2019

Put Me In The Story is a
registered trademark of Sourcebooks, Inc.
All rights reserved.

Published by Put Me In The Story,
a publication of Sourcebooks, Inc.
P.O. Box 4410, Naperville, Illinois 60567-4410
(630) 536-1104
www.putmeinthestory.com

Date of Production: July 2019
Run Number: 5015149
Printed and bound in Italy (LG)
10 9 8 7 6 5 4 3 2 1

MIX
Paper from
responsible sources
FSC® C023419
FSC www.fsc.org

Bestselling books starring your child!
www.putmeinthestory.com